DATE DUE

franks	

GAYLORD   PRINTED IN U.S.A.

Snickerdoodle's
Star-Spangled
Fourth of July!

By Clare Ham Grosgebauer

Illustrations by Karen Rissing

Based on the original character by Otis Ham
© 1980; revised edition 1986, 1999; text and illustrations ©2005 by Clare Grosgebauer.

ISBN 0-9741888-6-7
Library of Congress Control Number 2004099798

Printed in China.

Small Wonders Enterprises
12210 Fairfax Towne Center, #901
Fairfax, VA 22033
www.snickerdoodleforkids.com

SNICKERDOODLE™, a timeless tall tale hero from American folklore, is dedicated to parents, grandparents, and "little guys" of all ages who think big, love to laugh, and delight in sharing storytelling adventures together.

Originally introduced in the early 1900s by my grandfather, Otis Ham, SNICKERDOODLE, the "powerful pee-wee" who rides in a peanut, is a bold peacemaker and a goodwill ambassador for fantasy and fun. His mission is to bring smiles and laughter wherever he goes—to break through all barriers that cause people to take life too seriously.

In that spirit, I share SNICKERDOODLE's legacy and message—his "good news in a nutshell"—with you:

"Think BIG! Discover the small wonders within YOU!
You're never too little to make a difference!"

—Clare Ham Grosgebauer

At the Doodle farm, on the Fourth of July
Was a family picnic, with hot apple pie

And fried chicken and hot dogs and corn-on-the-cob,
And peanuts and popcorn for the whole Doodle mob.

The kids could play softball or go hide-and-seek,
And grown-ups went fishin' down at the creek.

As the flag was raised high up on the pole,
Uncle Yankee saluted and played a drum roll.

"It's dandy to live in the land of the free!"
Declared Uncle Yankee. "Don't you Doodles agree?"

Then foot-stompin', toe-tappin' music and song
Made the Doodle folks dance and whistle along.

Polly Wolly would strum and pick her banjo
While the crowd called out for songs we all know.

Polly Wolly loved bluegrass and folk songs and such,
And she sang them all great, with just the right touch.

A sweet country gal with a spirit so spunky

She'd even charm chickens whose behavior was funky!

But the best entertainment by far, of course,
Was a skating routine by Jerry the horse!

And that firehouse dog, SpitFire Jim, was really excited...
He was guarding the fireworks that would soon be ignited.

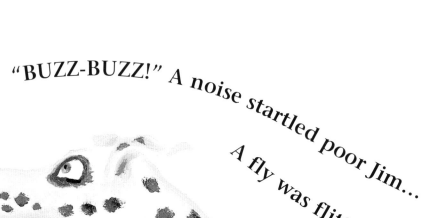

"BUZZ-BUZZ!" A noise startled poor Jim...

A fly was flitting and flirting with him!

"YIP-YIPE!" barked the dog, leaping so high—

He practically flew right into that fly!

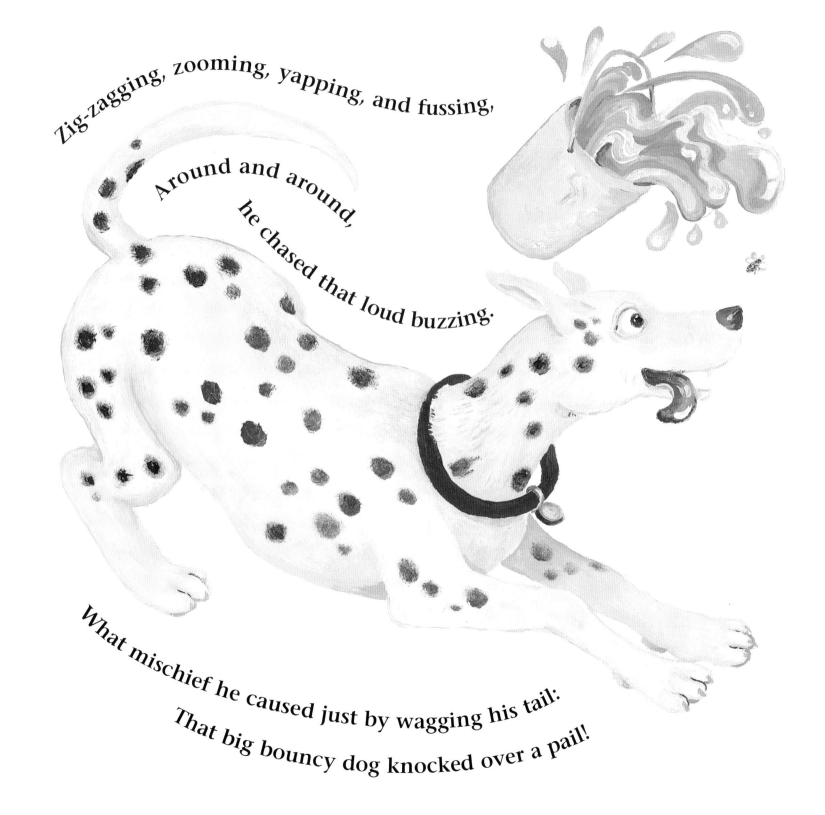

Zig-zagging, zooming, yapping, and fussing,

Around and around,

he chased that loud buzzing.

What mischief he caused just by wagging his tail:
That big bouncy dog knocked over a pail!

Water spilled out all over the place!
The fireworks got wet, much to SpitFire's disgrace.

"What's going on here? What's all the clatter?"
Asked Uncle Yankee, amidst all the chatter.

"Our fireworks are ruined," someone cried in dismay.
"That fire dog has spoiled our best holiday!

A Fourth without fireworks has no snap or sizzle—
A Fourth without fireworks doesn't fizz—what a fizzle!
A Fourth without fireworks is a dawn with no sun—
Yes, a Fourth without fireworks is surely no fun!"

"But wait! There's someone who'll save the occasion
And make it a cause for a real celebration,"

Said Uncle Yankee, with a twinkling eye...
SNICKERDOODLE can do it! Let's give him a try!"

That's right. SNICKERDOODLE! The "powerful pee-wee!"
He can solve any problem ... but where can he be?

Well, out at the creek, in his peanut boat,
SNICKERDOODLE was fishing and keeping afloat.

"What a wonderful day—not a cloud in the sky,"
Remarked SNICKERDOODLE. "Great Fourth of July!

But I'd better return to the picnic in town.
It'll be dark soon—the sun's going down.

But first I'll look for a little surprise
For our Doodle family's Fourth of July.

If I can find it,
it will be a delight...

Even better than fireworks
on a dark, starry night!

Once in these woods, at the edge of the park,

I saw something wild that glowed in the dark...

A STAR-SPANGLED CAT with a whimsical smile
And a big bushy tail and a proud, prancing style.

With colors and patterns and stripes geometric,
That glittered and gleamed with a glow most electric!

Here kitty-kitty! Come out and you'll see...
Here's a yummy fresh fish for your dinner with me."

"MEOW—WOWEE—YOW!" came a sound from a tree...
And down jumped the Star-Spangled Cat with such glee!

Her eyes were like stars, and her coat was all furry…
Her toes painted red, her voice soft and purry.

A magnificent cat with a holiday spark,
She was red, white, and blue—and she glowed in the dark!

"Just wait till they see YOU!" SNICKERDOODLE remarked.
"Whoever has seen a CAT glow in the dark?"

"What's so great about that?" she asked in surprise.
"So what if I glow and have stars in my eyes?

When I was a kitten, it really got frightening...
I was out in a storm and got struck by lightning!

Now, every night I glow red-white-and blue,
And 'meow' at the moon and the starry sky, too.

Other animals laugh at my colors so bright...
They say it's not natural to radiate light!

So, I live in these woods,
and I do all right...
I come out to this creek
to go fishing at night."

"But you are so SPECIAL—you ought to be proud
Of your own unique way to stand out from the crowd."

Said SNICKERDOODLE. "Come, share your glow
With some folks who will love you. C'mon now, let's go!"

"PUTT-PUTT!" went the peanut SNICKERDOODLE was driving.
With the Star-Spangled Cat he'd soon be arriving.

The cat pranced behind him, and then hid from sight.
As they reached the farm, it was almost twilight.

"Here's SNICKERDOODLE!" the crowd cheered a cheer.
"At last! We're so glad you are finally here!

We have no fireworks—they all got wet!
This is a Fourth we will never forget!"

"That's right," SNICKERDOODLE
said with a wink...

You won't forget it...
but what do you think

About this surprise I've brought for tonight...
It's a STAR-SPANGLED CAT. A special delight!"

Out jumped the cat and made a low bow.
It purred a soft purr and meowed a meow.

"A red-white-and-blue cat! How simply exotic!"
Declared Uncle Yankee. "She's so patriotic!"

"And look!" said someone, in a voice strong and clear,
"A parade of cats is marching through here!"

There were curious cats, all in a line—
Yellow ones, black ones, and striped ones so fine.

Each one played an instrument in the cat band.
Some tooted, some fiddled. (One did a handstand!)

And each one pranced to its own special beat—
Some marched on tiptoe, some on four feet.

"Play 'Stars and Stripes,'" yelled the crowd, "Please do!"
So the Star-Spangled Cat brought out her kazoo...

And conducted the cats in a concert so grand,
That everyone cheered for the kitty-cat band!

"It's getting dark now. I have an idea,"
Said SNICKERDOODLE. "SpitFire, come here.

You still have a chance to make this night fun...
If you'll do as I say... Good dog, now run!"

WHIZ-BANG! Jim zipped to the firehouse and back.
In his mouth was a box all shiny and black.

Inside it were candles for everyone.
"Let's light up the night and continue our fun!"

Said SNICKERDOODLE. "The line forms here.
So come light your candle and share some good cheer."

The Star-Spangled Cat was the first one in line
To show all the folks how to let their light shine.

SNICKERDOODLE just smiled. ("It was sheer inspiration
To rely on a cat for illumination!")

What a radiant brightness lit up the sky,
As the Star-Spangled Cat saved the Fourth of July!

Think Big!

SNICKERDOODLE'S™ BIG Message for Little Guys

I'm called "Snickerdoodle!" Yes, that's my name.
To "little guys" everywhere I'm here to proclaim:

Your courage, your spirit—not muscles and might—
Will vanquish all villains and whisk them from sight.

For the power of love is always far greater
Than the mask of meanness on the face of a hater.

And the power of truth melts boasting and lies
And outsmarts a bully—gives him a surprise!

The power behind you is much stronger by far
Than whatever confronts you—
IF YOU KNOW WHO YOU ARE!

Yes, real power shines within you—
makes you brave, makes you wise...
You can "zap" any problem in spite of its size!

And humor's a powerful weapon, you know.
It can topple a tyrant and befuddle a foe.

It can tickle a tycoon, make a giant guffaw,
Cause a chieftain to chuckle, and bemuse an outlaw.

Yes, humor heals hurts and divisions and strife...
If you want to be happy, then laugh all your life!

So, if a big tough guy crosses your path,
Surprise him with kindness—or be a friend, make him laugh!

Dare to make peace! The world needs your smile
To stretch across oceans, mile after mile.

And if you are small and think you can't win,
Just remember you're stronger than ten thousand men

Who ACT like they "know-it-all," (but really know "zero")...
You're a powerful pee-wee—a REAL superhero!